A Kitten Called Tiger

Other titles by Holly Webb

The Hounds of Penhallow Hall:

The Moonlight Statue

Winter Stories:

The Snow Bear
The Reindeer Girl
The Winter Wolf

The Storm Leopards
The Snow Cat

Animal Stories:

Lost in the Snow
Alfie all Alone
Lost in the Storm
Sam the Stolen Puppy
Max the Missing Puppy
Sky the Unwanted Kitten
Timmy in Trouble
Ginger the Stray Kitten
Harry the Homeless Puppy
Buttons the Runaway Puppy
Alone in the Night
Ellie the Homesick Puppy
Jess the Lonely Puppy
Misty the Abandoned Kitten
Oscar's Lonely Christmas
Lucy the Poorly Puppy
Smudge the Stolen Kitten
The Rescued Puppy

The Kitten Nobody Wanted
The Lost Puppy
The Frightened Kitten
The Secret Puppy
The Abandoned Puppy
The Missing Kitten
The Puppy who was Left Behind
The Kidnapped Kitten
The Scruffy Puppy
The Brave Kitten
The Forgotten Puppy
The Secret Kitten
A Home for Molly
Sammy the Shy Kitten
The Seaside Puppy
The Curious Kitten
Monty the Sad Puppy
The Homeless Kitten

Maisie Hitchins:

The Case of the Stolen Sixpence
The Case of the Vanishing Emerald
The Case of the Phantom Cat
The Case of the Feathered Mask

The Case of the Secret Tunnel
The Case of the Spilled Ink
The Case of the Blind Beetle
The Case of the Weeping Mermaid

A Kitten Called Tiger

Holly Webb
Illustrated by Sophy Williams

For Angel and Poppy – two adventurous cats!

www.hollywebbanimalstories.com

STRIPES PUBLISHING
An imprint of the Little Tiger Group
1 The Coda Centre, 189 Munster Road,
London SW6 6AW

A paperback original
First published in Great Britain in 2017

Text copyright © Holly Webb, 2017
Illustrations copyright © Sophy Williams, 2017
Author photograph copyright © Nigel Bird

ISBN: 978-1-84715-788-1

A CIP catalogue record for this book is available
from the British Library.

Printed and bound in the UK.

10 9 8 7 6 5 4 3 2 1

Chapter One

"Ava! Come on, wake up. Look at this!" Mum held up her phone in front of Ava's nose and Ava squinted at the photo on the screen sleepily. Then she sat bolt upright in bed and grabbed the phone. Ever since her parents had agreed to getting a kitten, Ava had been scanning the local animal shelter's website and checking the noticeboard in the supermarket. But no one seemed to have any kittens in need of homes – until now.

"Oh! They're gorgeous! Mum, are they real? I mean, are they for sale? Can we go and see them?" The photo showed a litter of kittens snuggled up in a cardboard box – it wasn't a very big one but they'd obviously all decided it was the best place to sleep ever. Ava was almost sure there were four but it was quite hard to count them…

"Yes, they're real and, yes, we can go and see them. Rosie, the lady who owns them, put their picture on Facebook and she said she's free this weekend if people want to visit. I've sent her a message to see if we can go round today. Your auntie Jade sent me their picture – Rosie's a friend of hers. Auntie Jade said she thought of you as soon as she saw them!"

"They're so little and fluffy..." Ava cooed, stroking the phone screen with her finger. Then she sighed as the picture disappeared. "Oops! Sorry, Mum, I'm still half asleep. I just wanted to stroke them!"

Mum smiled as she took back the phone. "I love the ginger and white one – but the stripey kitten's gorgeous, too. I think we might have a really hard time choosing. Oh, look! Rosie's messaged me back, asking if we can come round at about ten o'clock. Ooooh, I don't know, Ava, what do you think? It's a bit early for a Saturday, isn't it?"

Mum laughed as Ava leaped out of bed, flinging off the duvet. "You think we can, then? We've got to get Lucy and Bel up, remember. And your dad's still asleep."

"We've only got two hours!" Ava squeaked. "Wake him up now, Mum! And tell Lucy and Bel we're going to see some kittens. They'll be out of bed the fastest you've ever seen, I promise!"

"Hurry up," Ava groaned. "There's the house, look, number twenty-two. Lucy, you don't need to bring your toy cat, we're going to see *real* kittens…"

"They will like my toy cat," her sister said firmly, gathering up her toy cat and her handbag and all the cat's clothes, and clambering down from her car seat. Lucy was only just three – Mum and Dad had said they'd think about getting a family pet once she was old enough to understand that a kitten wasn't another toy for her to play with. Ava had been looking forward to Lucy's birthday more than her own.

Ava's middle sister, five-year-old Bel, had run on ahead and was trying to undo the latch of the garden gate.

She was just as excited as Ava was. Neither of them had been able to eat any breakfast, and they'd watched Dad and Lucy ploughing through their Weetabix with disbelief.

"OK." Dad locked the car and led Lucy over to the gate. "Let's go!"

Bel finally managed to unlatch the gate and the front door opened as they walked up the path. A lady in a stripey T-shirt waved at them. "I saw you coming. I'm Rosie." She scooped up a silvery tabby cat who was trying to escape round her legs. "And this is Moppet. She's the kittens' mum."

"She's beautiful," Ava's mum said.

"She really is," Rosie agreed. "Come on in. Moppet's too young to have kittens, to be honest. She was a stray. She kept coming into the garden and in the end I adopted her. I didn't know I was getting five cats instead of one!"

"Oh, wow…" Ava sighed. It sounded like a dream come true to her.

"Anyway, come and see the kittens. They're in the kitchen."

Ava could feel her heart thumping with excitement as they walked through the hallway. The kitchen door was closed and Rosie opened it carefully, obviously trying not to bump into any kittens on the other side.

"Oh! Oh! A kitten!" Bel squealed as a little furry face popped round the edge of the door.

The kitten disappeared at once and Mum shushed Bel gently. "Sweetheart, remember what we talked about. You've got to be quiet round the kittens. If you shout, you'll scare them."

Bel nodded but Ava could tell that she was so excited she wasn't really listening. Ava swallowed hard as Rosie opened the door all the way. There seemed to be a bubble of nervousness stuck in the top of her throat. She had been daydreaming about this moment for so long!

The kittens seemed to have taken over Rosie's kitchen. There were cat toys everywhere, a cosy basket sat next to the radiator, and a huge kitten climbing frame made of scratching posts and carpeted hidey-holes was squashed up next to the kitchen table. As they all went in, a small ginger kitten looked up from licking the butter off a piece of toast.

Rosie put Moppet down and sighed. "That was my breakfast," she told the kitten, lifting it off the table. "You've had yours." She looked round at Ava and her family. "They're lovely but they get everywhere." Then she frowned.

"Hang on. How many kittens can you see?"

Ava laughed. Now that she could actually see the kittens, the strange feeling inside her had disappeared. "Three," she told Rosie. "The one who was licking your toast…"

"There's another ginger one over there on the climbing frame," Bel said.

"And there's a tabby kitten by the door," Ava added, peering round the table to see properly. The tabby kitten was playing with a fluffy rabbit that was nearly as big as it was, rolling over and over on the floor.

"There ought to be four," Rosie said, scanning the kitchen. "We're missing one. There's another tabby kitten – and honestly, it's always him!"

Ava crouched down to check under the table but there was only the ginger kitten, still licking his buttery whiskers. Then, as she stood up, Ava spotted the tip of a stripey tail on top of the bookcase. "Is that him?" she asked Rosie, pointing. "Behind those photographs?"

"How did he get up there?" Dad laughed. "That's a huge jump for such a small cat."

Rosie shook her head, smiling. "I didn't think any of them could get up there. But I suppose if he went from the climbing frame to the table, to the edge of the sink and then scrabbled up the curtain… This whole kitchen is like a playground for kittens. But he's definitely the most adventurous!"

"Hello," Ava whispered to the kitten as he eyed her round the side of the photo frame. "Are you stuck?" The kitten looked so funny with his head sticking out one end of the frame and his tail the other. He mewed at her and edged a little further out from behind the photo. But there wasn't much room and he nudged into a vase that was standing behind him, making it wobble dangerously.

"Oh!" Ava said worriedly. "Come on, kitten. You're going to get squished in a minute." She reached up to lift him out from behind the photo frame and then looked uncertainly at Rosie. Was it OK to pick the kitten up?

Rosie nodded at her. "Can you reach?

Just lift him down from there."

Ava slipped both hands round the kitten's middle, hoping she wasn't scaring him. But she thought he actually looked quite grateful to be rescued. He didn't wriggle at all and she snuggled him against her cardigan, loving the feel of his warm fur and his squidgy kitten tummy.

"Oh, he's very handsome!" Mum said, coming over to look. "So stripey!"

"He's the stripiest cat I've ever seen," Ava agreed, looking down at the kitten. He was a beautiful golden brown colour, with black stripes running down his sides and fat black rings all along his tail. Ava had seen tabby cats before, of course, but never one with such perfect stripes.

"He's what's called a mackerel tabby," Rosie said. "Like the fish – they have stripes, too."

"He looks more like a tiger," Mum said. "The way his stripes match on both sides."

Ava giggled as the kitten scrabbled his way up her cardigan and climbed on to her shoulder. She knew he was probably just trying to get up high, so that he could see what was going on with all these strange people in his kitchen but it felt like he belonged with her somehow.

"Mum," she whispered. "Do you think… Could we have this one?"

Lucy stood up to see. She'd been trying to get the ginger kittens to look at her toy cat but they weren't very interested. "What's his name?" she asked Rosie.

"Oh, well, I tried not to name them, because I knew they'd be going to new owners," Rosie explained. "But in my head I've been calling him Adventure Kitten."

"He sounds like a superhero!" Ava said.

"I think he's called Tiger," Lucy said, nodding her head. "Let's take him home now."

"Oh, Lucy, we haven't decided yet," Mum said, but she was smiling.

"And don't forget, we need to go and buy a cat carrier and a basket and, oh, lots of things! Although he *is* lovely…"

"And Tiger would be a great name," Dad said. "Bel? Ava? What do you think?"

Bel reached up to stroke the kitten's tiny paws and smiled. "Even his paws are stripey."

Ava nodded, just a little, so as not to shake the kitten around too much. "It's perfect! He looks just like a tiger and he's as brave as one, too."

Chapter Two

When the carrier was set down at last and the wire door swung open, Tiger didn't move. He wasn't sure what was outside the carrier but he knew it wasn't his home. It smelled different. There was no comforting smell of his mother and the other kittens.

"Why isn't he coming out?" Bel said, crouching down.

"He's probably frightened," Mum explained. "This is all really strange for him."

"Should we try the cat treats? The ones Rosie said he liked?" Ava suggested, opening the kitchen cupboard.

Tiger took a step closer to the open wire door as he heard the crinkle of the foil packet. He could smell the treats, too – the delicious fishy ones. Even though he was still scared, he padded forwards another couple of steps and peered through the wire bars. Yes, there was the packet. His whiskers twitched and he eyed the girl holding the treats.

"Come on, kitten!" Lucy wriggled away from Mum and bounced towards the cat carrier. Tiger heard her voice and the thud of her footsteps and retreated back inside the carrier.

"Luuu-cy!" Ava snapped and then wished she hadn't when her little sister's face crumpled. "You have to be really gentle," she added, but Lucy had already burst into tears.

"Maybe we should give Tiger some time to come out by himself," Dad suggested. "I know you all want to play with him but he's nervous. Why don't we put on a DVD?" He picked up Lucy for a cuddle and led Bel out of the kitchen but Ava hesitated. Surely *she* could stay? Tiger liked her – he'd let her lift him off the bookshelf the day before and he'd seemed happy for her to hold him then. She looked pleadingly at Dad but he shook his head. "It isn't fair otherwise, Ava," he pointed out. "And there'll be loads of time to play with him."

Mum put an arm round her shoulders. "We'll give Tiger time to explore a little by himself, then we'll all go and see how he's doing. Anyway, don't you have to do your literacy homework, Ava? How long should that take you, twenty minutes? If you get it out of the way now then you'll have the rest of the afternoon free to play with Tiger."

Ava nodded and sighed. Mum was right about the homework. But why did Lucy and Bel always have to mess things up?

Tiger's ears twitched as the kitchen door clicked shut. He could still smell those cat treats. He crept to the carrier door and peered round it. There was a scattering of treats on the floor and they smelled so good. He stepped out and then started to crunch up the treats, looking around carefully between each bite. But there were only a few and they were gone in seconds. He looked uncertainly back to the carrier. He knew he was safe in there but he didn't like it much. Now that the kitchen was quiet, he wanted to explore.

He jumped up on to a kitchen chair and then the table. He liked to be high up, to see what was going on. He prowled across the table and eyed the window above the sink. The main window was mostly closed but there was a smaller window at the top and that was open. Just then, a bee looped in through the window from the garden. Tiger watched it with interest, not really sure what it was. He crouched down a little, wondering if he could pounce on the bee from where he was. It zigzagged round the kitchen and as it swooped back over the table he followed it, his tail twitching with excitement.

Tiger balanced at the very edge of the table, trying to swipe at the bee with his paw. But he just couldn't get close enough. Then the bee stopped for a rest, perched on the kitchen wall. Tiger hopped back on to the chair and down to the floor. He would creep up on it and pounce! Stealthily he padded across the tiles and then he launched himself at the bee.

The bee flew away, buzzing frantically, and Tiger turned his head to watch. He'd missed it by miles. Then he looked down and flexed his claws rather worriedly. They were firmly stuck in the thick wallpaper. He was halfway up the kitchen wall and he wasn't quite sure how he'd got there...

Ava peeped round the kitchen door, wondering where Tiger was. She had rushed through her homework – she was sure Mrs Atkins wouldn't be impressed.

"I hope he's come out of the cat carrier," Mum said, looking over her shoulder. "But I can't see him. I'm surprised he's so shy – he seemed really daring at Rosie's house. He was definitely the most adventurous of the four."

"Mum! Look!" Ava pointed across the kitchen at the wall, next to the fridge. Mum was always saying that she wanted to change the wallpaper, she thought it was too bright and plasticky-looking but Ava liked it. The paper was yellow, with a bright pattern of jam jars on it. Right now, though, halfway up there was a little stripey kitten.

"How did he get up there?" Mum gasped.

"He must have climbed up," Ava giggled. "I suppose the paper's squishy enough that he can stick his claws in. Poor Tiger! Are you stuck? Shall I get you down?" She walked slowly over to the wall. "How long have you been up there, silly boy? What did you do that for, hey?"

"Just be careful, Ava," said Mum. "Don't pull at him, it might hurt his claws."

Ava put one hand under Tiger's

bottom and tried to lift his front paws up a bit to unhook the claws.

"How is he?" Dad asked, putting his head round the door. "Settling in OK?"

Mum sighed. "You could say that. Look!"

Dad laughed. "Wow! That's one way to get rid of that wallpaper! Can you get him off there, Ava?"

"His claws are stuck right in," Ava said worriedly. "I can't lift his paws away and he's so panicked he's just clinging on. At least I'm holding him up now, so it's not like he's hanging there by his claws… What are we going to do? Should we call Rosie?"

Dad shook his head. "Just a minute, I've got an idea." He reached out and gently rubbed the top of Tiger's closest paw. The kitten looked round at him, his ears laid back, and his eyes wide and anxious-looking.

"What are you doing, Dad?" Ava asked.

"My mum did this when our cat climbed the back of the sofa and got stuck. Our old grey cat, Smokey – remember, Grandma Shirley showed you his picture."

Ava nodded. Her gran loved cats – she'd had several and Ava had seen photos of all of them. Smokey was the beautiful grey long-haired cat that Dad's family had owned when he was about Ava's age.

"It's working," Ava whispered as Tiger relaxed his claws and his paw came away from the wallpaper with a little popping noise. "Do the other paw, Dad!"

Dad rubbed Tiger's furthest paw and it happened even quicker this time. Tiger was free – his hind paws hadn't been stuck in nearly as deeply. Ava lifted him away from the wall and put him down carefully on the floor.

The kitten stalked away, shaking his ears crossly, and Ava pressed her hand across her mouth, trying not to laugh. "I think he's embarrassed that he got stuck," she whispered to Dad. "He's pretending it didn't happen!"

"I hope his paws are all right," Mum said, leaning sideways to look at the way Tiger was walking. "He's not limping, is he?"

"No, I think he's fine." Ava crouched down to check and Tiger looked round at her curiously. "Hey, Tiger. You're OK, aren't you? No sore paws?"

Tiger padded up to her and dabbed his nose against her knee.

Dad smiled. "Maybe that was a thank you."

Chapter Three

"Mum, where's Tiger?" Ava dashed out into the garden, where her mum was planting some cuttings. Ava's best friend Jess's dad worked as a gardener and he'd given them to Mum at school the day before.

"Isn't he in the kitchen? He was asleep in his basket a few minutes ago. I think he was worn out after you girls waved that feather toy at him for so long." Mum stood up, taking off her gardening gloves.

"He's definitely not. I came down to check on him after I'd finished my maths homework." Ava looked around the garden worriedly. "He didn't slip out after you, did he? He's not supposed to go outside yet!"

"I'm sure he didn't." Mum was silent for a moment. "I wonder where your sisters are…?"

Ava wheeled round and hurried back into the house. Lucy and Bel had been in their room, she'd heard them giggling. But they knew Tiger was supposed to stay in the kitchen for the first few days! She bounded up the stairs and burst into their bedroom.

"Go away! We're busy!" Lucy said crossly but Bel looked nervous. She put a doll's blanket over something in front of her – something that was moving!

"You've got Tiger up here!" Ava cried. "You have! You know he's supposed to stay in the kitchen – we've not even had him for a day!"

Tiger peered out from underneath the blanket and Ava gasped.

They'd been dressing him up. A doll's sock was falling off one of his front paws and there was a hat balanced on one twitching ear.

Ava scooped him up and cuddled him against her. "You mustn't do that! He's not a toy!"

"How come you get to play with him and we don't?" Bel demanded. "We were just having fun. He's our kitten, too."

"You can play with him properly, with cat toys! But you shouldn't dress him up like a doll." Ava slipped the sock off his paw – the hat had fallen off already.

"Give him back!" Lucy whined.

Bel stamped her foot. "You're not taking him, it isn't fair!"

"Oh yes, she is," Mum said from the doorway. "You knew he wasn't allowed to come upstairs yet. And what's this about dressing him up? Take Tiger back to the kitchen, Ava, I need to talk to Bel and Lucy."

Ava carried Tiger downstairs, stroking him gently. "I bet you wish you could go back to Rosie's house, where everybody was sensible," she whispered. "I can't believe my stupid sisters were dressing you up. They were probably going to put you in the doll's pushchair, weren't they?"

Tiger nuzzled under her chin. He hadn't liked Lucy and Bel pulling him around, although he had got to explore their room while they argued over which clothes to put on him and that had been interesting. So many things to clamber around and sniff and investigate. But he liked Ava's calm, gentle voice, and the way she was stroking his back over and over.

Ava sat down at the kitchen table, holding Tiger in her lap. She wasn't holding him tight, and she was expecting him to leap down from her knee and go and find somewhere to hide. Probably he'd want to tuck himself away inside his basket – it was one of those soft furry igloo ones, so he had his own little cave to snuggle in. But he stayed, kneading up and down on her leg with his needle-sharp claws.

"It's a good thing I've got jeans on," she whispered to him. "Are you OK? You're not still scared?"

Tiger turned himself round slowly and then settled down into a little heap on her lap. He looked around and spotted his feather toy lying on the floor close to his basket. Perhaps Ava would wave it for him some more? Then he slumped down again. No. He was too sleepy…

Ava watched him, a huge smile on her face. He was going to sleep – on her lap. Surely that meant he was happy, even after Lucy and Bel had been so awful.

Mum had explained to Bel and Lucy again that Tiger was only little and needed time to get used to them all. And that kittens never, ever, ever wanted to be dressed up. Ava wasn't totally sure that her little sisters understood, though. Lucy definitely thought Tiger was a new and improved sort of teddy. Ava wasn't sure what to do – maybe Lucy wasn't old enough for a pet, after all? But if she said that to Mum and Dad, they might agree with her and decide to take Tiger back!

"I'm going to tell Miss Daniels all about Tiger," Bel said, swinging her book bag round and round as she and Ava waited for Mum and Lucy in the front garden. "And everybody in my class." She stopped suddenly. "I could take in Tiger for Show and Tell!"

"No!" Ava yelped.

"He wouldn't like it, Bel," Mum said, locking the front door. "He'd be scared. But you could take in a photo?"

Bel was about to argue when she caught sight of one of her friends coming down the road with her mum and started waving. "Mia!"

Ava waved, too – her friend Jess was Mia's big sister and they all often ended up walking to school together.

"We've got a new kitten!" Bel told Mia proudly.

Jess looked surprised. "Have you really?" she asked Ava. "I didn't know you'd found one!"

"We went to see a litter of kittens on Saturday and we brought him home yesterday. He's called Tiger."

"Oh, lucky you…" Jess sighed. "I love our cats but they're both a bit old and doddery. It'd be great to have a kitten to play with."

"You can come and play with Tiger," Ava said. "Oh, hi, Megan!" Ava smiled as their next-door neighbour came out of her garden gate and then crouched down to stroke her dogs, Charlie and Max. "Are you going for a walk?" Ava loved the dogs. She sometimes went with Megan to walk them.

Charlie and Max wagged their feathery tails and yapped with excitement as all five girls made a fuss of them – even Lucy reached over from her pushchair to stroke their ears.

"We've got a kitten," Bel told Megan.

"I wonder if Charlie and Max can smell that? They're very excited. Come on, you two. We're a bit late this morning, we've only got time for a quick walk before I have to get to work," Megan told the girls. "Have a good day at school!"

"Bye!" Ava and Jess led the way round the corner to the alleyway that went past the woods. It went almost all the way to their school and Lucy's nursery. It was a bit wild, with overgrown hedges and nettles and other weeds growing up round the big trees, but because there were no cars, it meant she and Jess could walk on ahead and their mums didn't mind.

"Oooh, look, blackberries!" Jess reached into the bush to pick a couple and passed one to Ava. "So, is Tiger ginger with stripes?"

"No, he's brown – golden brown, with really black stripes. And the tip of his tail's black, too, like he dipped it in a pot of paint."

"Awww… Is he cuddly? I suppose he's a bit shy still."

"He was when he arrived," Ava agreed. "But he loves playing so much, he forgets to be nervous around us. And he's really adventurous! When we first saw him at his old house he was on top of a bookcase and yesterday he climbed up the kitchen wallpaper and got stuck!"

Jess giggled. "He sounds like he's going to get into trouble!"

Ava nodded. "I know. I love it that he's so bouncy and full of energy but I'm a bit worried about what he might do next!"

Chapter Four

"Look, Tiger." Ava put her hand through the cat flap and wiggled it about. Now that the kitten had had all his vaccinations, he was allowed to go outside. Ava couldn't wait. She really wanted to see Tiger out in the garden for the first time. She was sure he was going to love having more space to explore.

Jess had been right about the kitten being trouble. Tiger already went everywhere in the house – and that meant *everywhere*. He seemed to be able to squeeze into the smallest space and scramble up the tallest piece of furniture. He'd even managed to jump from the bookcase in Ava's bedroom to the top of her bedroom door. Then he'd sat there, looking a bit confused, as if he wasn't quite sure what he was meant to do next. Dad had lifted him down but Ava had a feeling it wouldn't be long before he tried again. Tiger just seemed to love being high up.

Ava let the cat flap bang shut again and looked at Tiger. He didn't seem to be getting it. He stared back at her.

He wasn't sure if this was some new sort of game. Ava was good at playing with him – she would roll a ball around for ages, or bounce his cat-dancer toy up and down. But now all she seemed to want to do was bang at this strange hole in the door.

Suddenly his ears pricked up and his whiskers twitched. He had caught a whiff of fresh air floating through the cat flap. The scent of outside, where he hadn't been allowed to go. He'd tried to get out, of course, hovering behind people as they went into the garden and sneaking after them, but they always caught him. He'd even got as far as the back step once, when Lucy nearly fell over and Mum was paying attention to her instead of watching the door. But then Mum had scooped him up while he was still staring out at the open stretch of grass.

"Come on, Tiger! You can go out," Ava told him, lifting the flap right up. "It's your own special door. Charlie and Max have one just like it, so they can get out while Megan's at work."

Tiger crept up to the cat flap and then jumped back as he saw Lucy peering through it from the garden.

"When's he coming out?" she demanded.

"He was about to!" Ava said. "You scared him!"

Lucy stomped away and Tiger poked his nose through the flap, looking out at the garden. It smelled so good, and he could hear birds scratching and fluttering in the bushes by the back door. He twitched his tail and hopped suddenly through the flap – so suddenly that Ava squeaked in surprise, and had to scramble up and open the door to follow him.

"He's out," she called to Mum, who was pushing Bel on the swing. "Look at him!"

Tiger prowled along the patio, stopping every few steps to sniff at a leaf or watch an ant scurrying between his paws. Then he walked into a patch of bright autumn sunlight, feeling its warm glow on his fur. He sat down for a moment, closing his eyes and letting the warmth soak in. Then he lay down and rolled over, his paws in the air. He blinked lazily as a bee buzzed past but couldn't be bothered to leap up and chase it.

Mum laughed. "He looks blissed out."

"It's good, isn't it?" Ava said, sitting down next to Tiger. "And now you can go out whenever you like," she told him.

"Not for too long this first time, though," Mum said. "Remember what it said in the cat care book. We need to take him back inside for his tea, so he learns that it's a good thing to come back home. We don't want him to wander off and get lost. And we'll need to keep the cat flap locked when we're not around, at least to start with."

Ava nodded. "I don't think he's big enough to get out of the garden yet, though. Megan's walls are too high and there's no holes underneath, because she doesn't want Charlie and Max escaping. And there's the wall between our garden and the alleyway on the other side. Tiger's not big enough to jump on to that."

"I don't think it's going to be long," Mum murmured. "He's such a good climber."

"I know." Ava sighed.

"This is really nice, Gran." Ava nibbled a piece of popcorn and snuggled up next to Grandma Shirley. "We should do this more often!"

"Definitely," her gran agreed. "We just have to persuade your mum and dad. It's very special for them to have a day out together."

"Shh!" Lucy glared at them. "Don't talk!"

Ava and Gran exchanged a look. Because Lucy was the littlest, she seemed to think she had to be extra bossy.

"Where's Tiger?" Bel asked, in a whisper. "I wanted him to sit on me while we watch the film."

Ava smiled at her. "Do you want me
to go and get him? He's in his basket."

"Please!" Bel whispered back. Gran
was smiling, too – she loved Tiger.
She'd told Ava she thought he was the
cleverest kitten she'd ever seen.

Ava hurried into the kitchen but there
was no stripey kitten in the basket. She
looked around the room – she even
checked the top of the door, just in case.
Tiger seemed to find pawholds where

she couldn't even imagine them. He must have gone upstairs, she thought, or perhaps he was out in the garden. Now he'd been allowed out for a few weeks, they left the cat flap unlocked in the daytime so he could go out by himself. She opened the back door and leaned out, calling, "Tiger! Tiger!"

She'd expected that he would leap out of the bushes by the back door. He loved lurking in there, watching the birds hopping about in the branches.

"Tiger!" Ava called again. But there was no answering mew, only Charlie and Max barking in the garden next door. Barking a lot, actually, Ava thought, wondering what was the matter. Megan worked on Saturdays, in one of the department stores in town, so the dogs were on their own.

"Hey, Charlie! Hey, Max," she called over the wall. "Shh… What's wrong?"

It was as if the dogs didn't even hear her. They just kept on barking.

Ava bit her lip, suddenly worried. She dashed back indoors and up the stairs, checking all the bedrooms to see if Tiger was curled up on someone's bed. But he wasn't. Ava leaned out of Lucy and Bel's bedroom window, trying to look down into Megan's garden but the wall was in the way. She could only see the back end of the garden and she knew the dogs were nearer the house – she'd heard them close to the back door.

Ava dug her nails into her palms, trying to stop herself panicking. She didn't know that Tiger was in next-door's garden. How could he be? He wasn't big enough to get over that huge wall and there were no gaps that he could have squeezed through. It couldn't be Tiger that Charlie and Max were barking at.

Ava wasn't completely sure, though. Not sure enough.

Tiger had been right down at the bottom of the garden, stalking a blackbird. It had been cheeky enough to flutter down on to the grass right in front of him. The kitten had been so surprised he almost fell over his own paws but as soon as he realized what was happening, he sank into a hunting crouch. He had seen birds hopping about in the bushes before but never one so close up. He inched forwards, hardly breathing, creeping nearer and nearer. Then, all of a sudden, the bird spotted him and shot into the air with a frantic beating of wings. Tiger dived after it but the bird was too fast. It was gone before he landed, up into the scrubby lilac that grew against the wall.

Tiger scrambled after the bird, and it squawked furiously at him and fluttered away over the wall.

He looked up as it flew off, with his ears laid back. He had been so close. Tiger clambered the rest of the way up the lilac, on to the wall, but the bird had disappeared. Then he gazed around curiously. He had never climbed on to the top of the wall before. He was high up enough to see all along the garden – and into next-door's garden. A whole new place to explore!

He paced along the bricks, wondering if there were any other cats down there. A huge white cat had appeared in his own garden a couple of days before and hissed at him as though he wasn't meant to be there. He had been furious and scared all at the same time. But then Bel and Ava had come outside and started shouting, and the white cat had dashed away.

The new garden seemed quite still, so he sprang down on to the grass and began to wander about, sniffing curiously at the plants. He was just investigating the tiny pond next to the patio when there was a sudden bang, followed by an ear-splitting series of barks.

Charlie and Max came shooting out of their dog flap, barking so loudly that Tiger just froze. He stood perched at the edge of the pond, trembling in fright.

Tiger had seen the dogs before,
out of the window – he'd even heard
Charlie and Max when he was in his
own garden. But he hadn't known
they lived here! He hadn't realized
that this garden belonged to them.

Terrified, Tiger ran at last, racing
towards the gate.

Chapter Five

"Ava, are you all right?" Grandma Shirley called up the stairs.

"I can't find Tiger!" she said, dashing down to Gran. "And the dogs next door, they're barking like mad. Do you think Tiger could have got into their garden?"

Gran looked doubtful. "Surely not … with that big wall? But then, cats really are amazing climbers…"

"I know. I have to check, Gran, but I can't see over the wall from the back windows, I've tried."

Ava hurried out into the garden and looked up at the wall helplessly. She'd never be able to see over it. It was more than two metres tall. Ava drew in a deep breath – the wall was just too big. Tiger couldn't have jumped on top of it, could he? But then, he'd managed to jump on to her bedroom door… He might have managed it if he'd jumped on to something else first. She had to make sure.

"Gran, can you hold on to this chair for me?" Ava asked, pushing one of the garden chairs up against the wall. "I need to look over the top."

She stepped up on to the chair. "Oh no. That's no use – it's not tall enough." She was still a long way from seeing into next-door's garden.

"Oh, Ava, be careful," Gran gasped as she jumped down. "I don't want to ring your mum and dad and tell them I've had to take you to hospital with a broken leg!"

"I am being careful, Gran, I promise. But I have to see if Tiger is there…" Ava shuddered. "Charlie and Max are nice dogs, Gran, but listen to them.

They sound so fierce. Look, do you think you can help me push the table up against the wall? I can get on the chair, then the table and then I think I'll be able to see over the top."

Gran sighed. "I suppose there's not much else we can do. I'm so sorry, Ava, I really don't think I can climb up there."

"I'll be fine, Gran, honest. Here, just push this for me." Ava grabbed the edge of the metal table, dragging it towards the wall. "It's coming!" With Ava pulling and Gran pushing, the table bumped and juddered up against the wall.

"Why are you in the garden?" Bel was standing at the back door, with Lucy peeping round her.

"Oh! Go back inside, you two!" Gran sounded harassed.

"What are you doing?" Bel's bottom lip stuck out. She was going to cry, Ava realized.

"They won't go back in," Ava told Gran. "Not without having a real meltdown. We have to tell them what's going on." She turned to Lucy and Bel. "The dogs are barking a lot and I can't find Tiger. I think he might be in Megan's garden."

Bel stared at Ava, her eyes round with horror. "But they might eat him!"

"Tiger!" Lucy wailed. "I want Tiger!"

"I do, too," Ava said, stepping up on to the chair. "So that's why I'm climbing up here. Now, you have to be good and not cry."

Gran nodded. "Ava's right. Come out here, you two. I know you've only got your slippers on, it doesn't matter for once. You can help me hold the table so Ava doesn't wobble."

Lucy and Bel pattered out, and held on tightly to the edge of the table. It was clever of Gran to get them to help, Ava thought as she crawled cautiously up on to the table. Now they wouldn't whinge about being left out.

"Is he there?" Lucy gasped, as Ava balanced herself against the wall and stood up.

"I can't see yet." Ava peered over the top, looking anxiously round the garden. "Oh! Oh, Tiger!"

"He is there! Is he all right?" Gran called up. "Oh, be careful, Ava!"

"He's there but I don't know if he's all right," Ava said, her voice shaking.

Tiger was curled up in a tiny ball, right by Megan's back gate. Charlie and Max were standing over him, still barking. The gate was a solid one, with no gaps in it and hardly any space underneath. And it was high, too. It looked like Tiger hadn't been able to scrabble his way up and over – he was trapped.

"I don't think he's hurt," Ava called down. "Just really, really scared. But I can't tell for sure."

Max realized at last that someone else was invading his garden. He trotted over to the wall and barked at Ava.

Even though he was huddled up with his eyes closed, Tiger heard the difference in the barking. One of the dogs had gone! He opened his eyes a tiny bit and looked over.

Ava! She was there, looking over the wall! He tried to get up to run to her but the other dog leaned over him, barking even more fiercely, and Tiger huddled back down to the ground. He didn't dare move – he was frozen with fear.

"Oh, Tiger," Ava whispered. "Gran, I have to get him out! He's so scared, and Charlie and Max might hurt him."

"What about the lady next door –
when's she going to be back?" Gran
asked. "Do we have a phone number
for her?"

"The home number's in Mum's
address book but that's no good. She's
at work." Ava looked down at Gran.
"It'll be hours till she's back. Megan
works till about six on Saturdays, I
know she does because she told Mum
she doesn't like it." Ava leaned over
the wall again. "I'm coming to get you,
Tiger. I'll be back in a minute."

"Coming to get him? No, you are
not!" Gran said, sounding horrified.
"You can't get over there, Ava!"

"I'm not leaving him! Even if we
call Mum and Dad, that food fair they
went to is an hour away on the train.

We can't leave him that long, Gran.
The dogs…" Ava's voice wobbled.
"They're really friendly and nice
normally but you can hear how excited
they are. What if he scratches one of
them and they snap at him?"

Gran stared at her uncertainly and
then flinched as one of the dogs let
out another loud bark. "All right. I
suppose we do have to do something.
But I don't see what, Ava. You can only
just see over the wall – you can't get up
there and you certainly can't jump down
on to the other side. Then you'll be in
the garden with those fierce dogs!"

"They aren't fierce, Gran, honestly.
I see them almost every day with
Megan and I've even helped her
take them for walks. They're barking

because of Tiger, that's all."

"And how are you going to get back again?"

Ava scrambled down from the table. "Dad's ladder. I should have thought of it before. It's in the shed. I can climb up on to the top of the wall, and then pull it up after me and put it down on the other side. It'll be fine, Gran." Ava crossed her fingers hopefully behind her back. "I do stuff like this in gymnastics club all the time."

"Throwing ladders around?" Gran muttered. "Get the ladder, Ava, and let me see how stable it is. You won't have anyone to hold it on the other side. Oh, maybe I should just have rung your mother…"

Ava threw open the shed door and grabbed the ladder. Luckily it was right by the door and she didn't have to face the enormous spiders that lived in the shed. And it was lighter than it looked, too. She carried the ladder back down the garden and set it up by the wall.

Gran, Lucy and Bel caught hold of it, and Ava climbed up, trying to ignore the wobbling and creaking, and the thumping of her heart. "I'm going to climb on top of the wall now," she said, refusing to let her voice shake. "And then can you help me pull up the ladder, Gran?"

"Be careful," Bel called. "Please don't fall off, Ava!"

"I won't." Ava hugged the top of the wall and lifted her closest leg over so that she was sitting with one leg either side. Just like the beam at gymnastics, except a bit higher up, that was all… She reached down and pulled the ladder up behind, feeling grateful that it was so light.

"I'm coming, Tiger," she murmured, looking over at the huddled pile of brown fur by the gate. "Don't be scared. It's going to be OK."

The dogs were very confused. They had a cat in their garden and now somebody was climbing over the wall, too. They circled between Ava on the wall and Tiger by the gate, barking at both of them but wagging their tails at Ava – they knew her, even if she wasn't usually in their garden.

"Good dogs," Ava said, trying to sound calm. "Hi, Charlie. Good boy, Max. I'll be gone in a minute. I'm just coming to get Tiger. We'll both be out of here soon."

She rocked the ladder gently, trying to see if it was nice and steady – but Megan's patio was gravel, not solid paving slabs like in her garden, and the ladder kept shifting. Ava gritted her teeth and climbed on to it anyway. She wasn't giving up now. It swayed and wobbled, and Ava closed her eyes and jumped. The ladder fell over with a crash and there was a wail from the other side of the wall. Lucy and Bel were crying.

"Ava! Ava! What happened?" Gran called frantically.

"I just jumped off the last bit of the ladder. I'm fine, Gran, I promise. Tell Lucy and Bel I'm OK. Down, Charlie! Down, Max!" Ava hurried across the garden to the fence, the dogs getting under her feet as she ran.

"Poor Tiger!" She scooped him up and pressed her face against his soft coat. "Come on. We're getting out of here," she whispered to the little kitten. "I've got him, Gran!" she called.

She dashed back to the ladder, pushing it back close against the wall with her free hand. The dogs stood watching, occasionally waving their tails – they'd probably never had such an exciting afternoon, Ava thought.

Tiger wriggled a little, realizing that he was safely away from the dogs. He was with Ava. He was almost home! He didn't understand what had happened but the terror that had gripped him as the dogs chased him down the garden slowly began to slip away.

Ava reached up and gently placed him on top of the wall. Tiger stood there for a moment, gazing down at next-door's garden and the dogs. Then he looked back at Ava, as she cautiously climbed the ladder.

"Can you get back up?" Gran called.

"I'm coming," Ava said, as she reached the top of the ladder and pulled herself up on to the wall. "Oooh. Ow."

"Ava?" Bel cried anxiously.

"Don't worry. I just scratched my arms a bit." Ava gave Tiger a stroke and waved down to Gran and her sisters. "It's all OK!"

Chapter Six

Tiger's adventure in next-door's garden was going to become part of their family history, Ava realized. She told the story to Mum and Dad as soon as they got back. And then to Jess on the way to school on Monday, Mrs Atkins during registration and all her friends at break. When Dad came home that night he said he'd told everyone at work about her heroic rescue. Ava didn't feel very heroic, though. After she'd finally got back down the ladder, she'd suddenly started shaking. She never, ever wanted to go up one again.

Ava was pretty sure it wasn't going to be the last time they would have to rescue Tiger, either. But hopefully he wouldn't try getting into Charlie and Max's garden again, not after his huge scare.

The other good thing about Tiger's adventure was that it seemed to have made Bel and Lucy understand that Tiger had to be looked after and kept safe. Lucy was a little too young to understand properly but she was still big enough to run and tell someone if she saw Tiger out in the front garden, or on the wall between the garden and the alleyway. Ava felt like the three of them were a team.

Perhaps it was because everyone was watching out for him so carefully, or perhaps he was keeping to the safety of the house after having such a fright, but Tiger behaved beautifully all that week. He didn't get stuck anywhere. He was always around whenever anybody called for him. He didn't even sneak out into the front garden and worry Mum by gazing at the road.

But then on Sunday, exactly a week after his great escape, Tiger disappeared again.

Ava had been working on a project for school – it had to be in soon, so she spent all of Sunday afternoon drawing pictures of Mayan headdresses and copying out chocolate recipes. She didn't notice that she hadn't seen Tiger. Bel had a birthday party and Lucy was cross because she didn't. It wasn't until Dad started making dinner and got out the cat food to feed Tiger that everyone realized they had no idea where the kitten was.

"Ava? Is Tiger up there with you?" Dad called up the stairs.

Ava came out on to the landing. "No. I haven't seen him since lunchtime." She looked at her watch. "He hasn't come in for his tea?"

Dad smiled up at her. "I'm sure he'll turn up in a minute. Don't worry, Ava."

Ava went back to her project but she

couldn't concentrate. After spending ten minutes writing one sentence, she went downstairs. "Dad, is he back?"

"No," her dad admitted. "I went out in the garden and called, and I had a quick look around the front, too."

"Shall I go and check again?"

"All right, but don't go far. It's getting dark."

Ava let herself out of the front door and started to walk along the pavement, calling to Tiger. She hoped that any moment she'd see a little stripey cat racing along the road towards her.

"Ava, what are you doing out here?" Mum and Bel had pulled up in the car outside the house, and Ava hurried over to them.

"We can't find Tiger! Mum, shall I ring Megan's doorbell? Just to check he's not in her garden again."

"Let's do that," Mum murmured, following Ava up their neighbour's path, with Bel clinging to her hand.

Megan answered the door straight away, smiling until she noticed Ava's anxious face. "What's wrong, Ava? Oh no, the dogs haven't chased Tiger again, have they?" She looked down at Max and Charlie, who were bouncing about by her feet.

Ava had told Megan all about the rescue mission – Mum had taken her round the following day to say sorry for climbing over the wall. Megan had said it was an emergency and she would have done exactly the same. She said Ava was very brave and she'd given Mum a spare key to the gate in case it happened again.

"We can't find him!" Ava gasped. "Tiger's always back for tea, always!"

"Megan, you couldn't have a quick look in your garden, could you?" Mum asked.

"Of course. Here, you two, in here, come on." Megan shut the dogs into her living room. "I'll just go and see. Hold on a minute."

Ava waited, breathing fast. She

wasn't sure what she wanted Megan to say. If the dogs had chased Tiger again, he would be so scared. But if he wasn't in her garden, it meant that they had no idea where he was…

Tiger had jumped on to the wall between the garden and the alleyway. It was a jump that he'd only just got big enough to do – he had to leap on to the back of the garden bench and then up on to the wall, and it was a tough scramble. But once he was up there, he could walk along it all the way down the side of the house to the front garden and the street. Then he could sit on the wall and watch people and cars going past, or even jump down on to the pavement. There were all sorts of interesting smells out there and a tree in the garden next door that was always full of sparrows. Tiger had never caught a bird – but of course he was going to keep trying.

That afternoon the sparrows were particularly loud and they kept fluttering about in the bush outside Megan's house in a most fascinating way. Tiger hopped from Ava's front wall down on to Megan's and prowled along to be closer to the tree. But he wasn't quick enough, or quiet enough. The sparrows heard the little thump as he dropped down and they flew away, scolding shrilly.

Tiger stood on the wall, staring at the empty bush. Then he simply pretended that he hadn't been trying to chase the sparrows at all and leaped down on to the pavement.

He stalked along crossly, wondering if he could work out where the sparrows had fluttered away to. He was thinking about the birds and not paying that much attention to anything else.

"Hey!" All of a sudden, there was a strange hissing noise behind him, followed by a squeal and an angry shout. Tiger darted out of the way with a yowl of fright as a bike skimmed past him. The rider's leg brushed against the kitten, shoving him sideways. Tiger shot away down the pavement but he was so scared that he ran right past his house and into the alleyway. He'd never been down the path before but he didn't care. He just wanted to get away from the bike and the angry rider.

Tiger dashed along the alleyway but it didn't feel far enough. He had to go up. If he was up high, he would be safe. No one would be able to catch him. He leaped and scrambled up into one of the tall trees. Still shaking from fright, Tiger kept climbing, higher and higher. He had to get as far up as he possibly could.

At last he stopped, crouched on a branch right at the top of the tree. Trembling all over, he gazed out into the darkening night.

Chapter Seven

"No one's seen him at all?" Dad asked, as Mum and Ava came back in. He'd been putting Lucy and Bel to bed while Mum and Ava went out searching for Tiger.

"No. But it's eight o'clock. Ava needs to go to bed."

"I don't want to!" Ava protested. "Honestly, Mum, there's no way I

could sleep now, when we still don't
know where Tiger is."

"You've got school tomorrow. No,
Ava, I'm not arguing, it's bedtime. I
promise Dad and I will keep looking
up and down the street. We'll take
turns. And we've asked all the
neighbours, remember. If anyone sees
Tiger, they'll call us."

"He hasn't been missing that long,"
Dad pointed out. "Only a few hours,
since after lunch sometime."

"Dad! He never, ever misses tea!"
Ava pressed her hands to her eyes.
She'd been trying really hard not to cry
– she knew it wouldn't help – but she
was so tired and frightened. And if *she*
was frightened, how was Tiger feeling?
What if he was lost or hurt?

"I know some cats stay away for ages," she went on, her voice shaking. "But Tiger doesn't. He's still only little and he loves home! He does stupid things but he doesn't go off a long way away. He might be trapped somewhere. Or maybe he's been hit by a car!" She couldn't hold back her tears any more.

Mum pulled her into a hug. "Ava, sweetie. I know you're scared. But it's too soon to panic like this. Dad's right. Tiger will probably pop through the cat flap in an hour or so, looking like he's never been away. And you can't stay up any longer. Come on. Bed."

Mum shooed Ava up the stairs and she went to her room, dragging her feet all the way. She couldn't imagine that she'd ever sleep. She was far too worried. She put on her pyjamas and trailed into the bathroom to do her teeth, all the time straining her ears for the bang of the cat flap. It didn't come. She climbed into bed and lay there, crying silently into her pillow.

"Ava! Ava!"

She must have fallen asleep, Ava realized. If she hadn't, no one would need to be waking her up…

That was Bel, Ava thought sleepily. And there seemed to be something heavy weighing down her feet. She sat up, blinking. Her room was still dark but she could see, just a little, by the nightlight on the landing. "What's the matter? It's not time to get up…" she whispered.

"We're worried," Bel told her.

The strange heavy lump on Ava's feet turned out to be Lucy, sitting on the end of the bed. "Worried…" she echoed.

"About Tiger?" Ava sighed. "Me, too."

"You have to find him, Ava," Bel said seriously. "You rescued him from Charlie and Max. You climbed over the wall! I want him back. And so does Lucy."

"We'll look for him again tomorrow before school," Ava said, trying to sound confident. "I bet we'll find him."

"Do you *promise*?" Bel demanded.

"Um." Ava swallowed hard. How could she promise? But Bel and Lucy looked so scared. "I promise…" she whispered.

Tiger stretched and shivered. He was so cold, he ached. He had spent the night huddled up on his branch, sleeping every so often but then being shocked awake as he remembered the bike nearly running him over.

He desperately wanted to go back home to Ava and his family, and have them stroke him and snuggle up with him and make him feel safe. But he didn't dare go back down the tree, even though he felt so terribly hungry. It was starting to get light now – it felt like breakfast time, except that he'd missed his dinner so his stomach was doubly empty. He needed a drink, too…

Tiger gazed down through the
early morning mist. He
could just make out
the road from
up here. The
occasional car
zoomed past,
making him
shrink back
against the tree
trunk but they
never came anywhere
close. And there was no sign
of the man on the bike. Perhaps it was
safe to climb down now?

Tiger stood up cautiously. The cold
seemed to have made it harder to
know what he was doing – his paws
didn't feel quite right and he shook

as he tried to walk a little way along the branch. He dug in his claws and clung on, suddenly feeling the wind blowing through the tree and shaking the branches. Until now he had felt safe up in the tree, so far from everything else. He hadn't thought about getting down.

He had gone up the tree so fast, he hadn't really thought about anything at all, only escaping. Now that it was light, the ground seemed so far away and he realized that he was higher up than he had ever been before. Far higher up than he wanted to be. Tiger mewed in sudden fright, again and again. He was stuck.

Ava ran out of school, still pulling on her raincoat, with Jess chasing after her. She had spent the whole day watching the hands creeping round the classroom clock, desperate for home time, so she could go and search for Tiger again. Mum had promised that if he turned up, she would ring the office and get the school secretary, Mrs Marshall, to take a message down to Ava and Bel, saying that Tiger was back. There hadn't been a message, though. Ava had even gone to the office at lunchtime to check, just in case Mrs Marshall had been too busy to come to her class.

Mum had also explained to her teacher, Mrs Atkins, which was good. Otherwise Ava thought she'd probably have got into trouble, as she'd hardly done any work all day. She'd just been waiting and waiting.

She could see Mum and Lucy by the gate but Mum didn't look happy – she'd probably be jumping up and down and waving if it was good news.

"Did you ask the neighbours again?" Ava burst out, looking up at Mum anxiously.

"I did. Lucy and I went all the way up and down the street, and to the roads close by. And I rang the vet's but they hadn't seen him either. That's good news, Ava. It means –" Mum swallowed – "well, it means he hasn't been hit by a car and taken there."

Ava nodded, her eyes filling with tears again. She sniffed. "Yes. That's good."

Jess came hurrying up and gave Ava a hug. "We can look for him on the way home. I really want to help and my mum will, too. Mia's going for tea at Amy's house."

Ava's mum smiled at her. "Thanks, Jess. I'm sorry we didn't walk with you this morning. We were so late, I ended up dropping the girls in the car – we went looking for Tiger again before breakfast, you see." She sighed. "Not that you ate anything, Ava. Please tell me you ate your lunch? Dad told me you didn't have dinner last night, either."

"I ate a bit," Ava said. She had – a

tiny bit. She just didn't feel hungry.
There was too much worry inside her
to fit in food as well.

"There's Bel." Mum waved as Bel's
class came out into the playground.
Ava went over to the gate and stood
a little way away with Jess. She didn't
want to hear Mum explaining to Bel
that Tiger was still missing. She'd tried
so hard to be brave and to tell Lucy
and Bel that it was going to be OK –
but she was starting to think that it
wasn't going to be OK at all.

Tiger had watched people going along
the path all day long. He'd mewed,
hoping they'd look up and see him,

and help him get down. But it was a wet, windy day and the few people hurrying by hadn't heard the sad little noises up above. He was starting to feel desperate. Every time the wind gusted the tree shook, and the branch where he was perched swung up and down.

Where was Ava? Why had he ever gone out into the front garden in the first place? He should have just stayed safe at home with Ava and Lucy and Bel!

There were footsteps again now. But no one was going to hear him – they hadn't all the other times. Miserably he slunk back along the branch, right up against the trunk of the tree, trying to stay out of the wind.

The footsteps came closer – they were almost under the tree now. And then Tiger's ears pricked up as he heard a familiar voice.

"I'm sorry, Jess. I'm just so worried about him. If I cry in front of Bel and Lucy they'll be really upset. They think that because I rescued Tiger before, I'm going to be able to find him."

"We *will* find him," Jess said, giving Ava a quick hug. "I'll help you make some posters when we get back. He's probably stuck in someone's shed."

"Maybe…"

Tiger sprang up, forgetting for a moment to be scared of the swaying branch. He darted out as far as he could and mewed frantically for Ava.

Chapter Eight

Ava froze in the middle of the path. "I heard him! Jess, I heard Tiger mewing!"

Jess stopped, staring around. "Oh, wow! I heard him that time, too! Where is he, though? I can't see him."

Ava turned round slowly, listening for the mewing, trying to work out where it was coming from. She was almost certain it was Tiger – he was all right! At least, she hoped he was. He sounded scared.

"I can't see him. Oh! Jess, look! He's up there!" Ava pointed over to the tall tree by the side of the alley.

"Where?" Jess squinted up at the tree. "Are you sure?"

"Yes!" Ava's voice shook. She pointed again, impossibly far up into the branches. "Right at the top. Tiger! Tiger! He can see us!"

Tiger yowled loudly and started pacing up and down the branch.

Jess swallowed. "Do you think he's been there all this time? Is he stuck?"

"He must be. Mum! We found him!" Ava waved madly at her mum, who was just catching up with them, along with Jess's mum. "Bel, he's here!"

Bel ran over and Mum broke into a jog with Lucy's pushchair. "Up in the tree? I might have known he'd be stuck somewhere silly! Oh, Ava, I'm so relieved, well done…" Her voice trailed off as she looked up into the tree and saw how high up Tiger was. He was still walking up and down the branch, mewing down at them. "Oh, my goodness!"

"How are we going to get him down?" Ava asked, clutching her mum's arm. "I don't mind climbing trees but I don't think I can get up that far."

Mum shook her head firmly. "You're definitely not climbing. I don't want you stuck up there as well. We could call Dad but it'll take him quite a while to get back from work. I wonder if we could ring the fire brigade?"

"A fire engine?" Bel asked, hopping up and down excitedly.

"They couldn't get a fire engine down here," Jess's mum put in. "But Dave might be able to reach her if he used his long ladder."

Ava looked at her hopefully. Dave was Jess's dad and he had ladders for trimming trees. "Has he got a really tall ladder? We've only got a little one."

Jess's mum nodded, smiling at her. "He definitely has. And I'm pretty sure he said he was doing a garden down the road today. It's going to be all right, Ava." She pulled her phone out of her pocket. "Hey, love. Look, are you nearly done? You're in Fircroft Lane, aren't you? It's Ava and Bel's kitten, he's stuck up a tree in the alley by their house. Have you got your long ladder with you?" She listened for a moment and then said, "You're a star. See you in a minute." Then she patted Ava's shoulder. "It's OK. He was just finishing. He'll be here soon."

Tiger peered down through the branches at Ava. He wanted to get to her so badly but he didn't see how he could. Ava kept calling up to him. He loved hearing the sound of her voice. Surely she'd find a way to bring him down?

Then he saw someone else – a man, carrying a long ladder. Ava and the others rushed over to talk to him, and Tiger stared at them, wondering what was happening. Then the tree juddered as the ladder was pushed against it and Tiger gave a little mew of fright as he felt the branch shake again.

Tiger sank his claws tightly into the bark. The ladder was growing taller now, pushing up towards him.

Tiger was still jumpy from the incident with the bike and a whole night stuck up the tree on his own, and he hated the look of the metal thing that was getting closer and closer. What was going on? Why wasn't Ava coming for him?

Mewing, he started to edge back, out along the branch to the narrow end, shaking and bouncing in the wind. He had to get away before that metal thing reached him.

Jess's dad climbed back down the ladder, shaking his head. "It's no good. He's terrified, poor little thing. He's going further and further along the branch as I get closer to him. I don't want to risk it."

Ava's mum sighed. "Oh no. Thanks so much, Dave. Maybe I should try? Perhaps he'd be OK with someone he knew."

"Mum!" Ava stared at her. "You can't! You hate heights." Dad was always teasing Mum about it. She didn't even like the big slide at the funfair. "What about me?" Ava asked, swallowing her nerves. She really didn't want to climb another ladder, not after she'd almost fallen off that ladder a few weeks before. But someone had to get Tiger down.

Mum shook her head. "I don't want you going up that high! And how are you going to climb down again with a wriggly little kitten?"

"Tiger isn't wriggly when Ava carries him," Bel put in.

Ava nodded. "I've got a better idea, anyway. Why don't we get the cat carrier? If I put that on the branch, with cat treats in it, he'd definitely climb in. Then I could shut the door and pass it down to Jess's dad."

"That's actually a really good plan," Dave agreed. "I could climb up behind Ava and help her. The ladder's not strong enough for two adults on it at the same time but me and Ava should be fine."

Mum nodded slowly. "All right, if you reckon that will work. I'll run home and get the carrier and the cat treats."

It seemed like the longest five minutes ever. Ava held Bel's hand and they all took it in turns to call lovingly up to Tiger. But then, at last, Ava saw her mum come hurrying back.

"Right, Ava," Dave said, as Mum opened the treats and placed them inside the carrier. "You start climbing up. Your mum and Jess's mum are going to hold the ladder steady, and I'm going to climb up behind you with the carrier. I'll pass it to you when you're ready."

Ava nodded, trying to wriggle her fingers. They felt so cold and she knew it was only because she was nervous… But what if she slipped while she was climbing the ladder? It was twice as high as the garden wall, at least.

She just couldn't slip, that was all. She had to do it.

Slowly she put her foot on the first rung of the ladder and began to climb. She didn't look down at the ground or even up at Tiger. She just looked at the rungs in front of her and kept going.

"I'm coming up behind you now, Ava. Hold on tight and don't worry if you feel the ladder shaking!" Dave called.

"OK!" Ava called back, her voice odd

and high. The ladder *was* shaking and it was making her feel a bit sick.

"Ava, you're nearly there!" That was Bel's voice, sounding a very long way below.

"A couple more rungs, Ava." Mum called. "You're doing so well."

Ava lifted her face a little to look up at the branches and gasped as she saw Tiger for the first time since she'd started climbing. He was there, staring at her, and he looked so scared.

Suddenly Ava felt a tiny bit better. "Hey, Tiger," she murmured. "We're going to get you down." Carefully she went up two more rungs, so that she was right next to Tiger's branch. She definitely wouldn't have been able to carry the kitten back down, she thought, shivering a little.

"Here's the carrier," Dave said quietly. "Can you grab it? You'll have to let go with one hand. Take your time."

Ava nodded, and forced herself to loosen her fingers and reach down. She grabbed the handle and shakily pushed the carrier up on to the branch. There was a forked bit of branch sticking out and she wedged the carrier in it. Now she didn't have to hold on to it – otherwise she'd have to let go with both hands to open the door. The packet of cat treats was inside – Tiger's favourite flavour, she noticed, the fishy ones. Ava reached in and shook the scrunchy foil bag.

"How are you doing?" Dave called up.

"He's coming!" Ava cried.

Tiger had started edging back along the branch. It was going to work! His soft fur brushed against her arm as he climbed into the carrier, sniffing at the bag. Ava shut the door so quickly she almost caught his tail and then she turned the catch.

"He's in!"

"Brilliant! Pass him down to me then. Take it slow, Ava. The carrier's going to be heavy now."

Ava nodded, lifting the carrier and reaching down to pass it to Dave. She heard a worried little mew as the carrier moved. "It's OK, Tiger. We're going home," she whispered to him.

"Back down now, Ava. Nice and slow."

Ava wasn't sure how she ever got back down the ladder. She didn't even remember doing it. She was just there at the bottom, with Mum hugging her and saying she'd been so scared and she should never have let Ava go up there, and Bel telling her she was the best big sister ever, and Lucy moaning because no one was listening and she'd dropped her toy cat.

Ava crouched down in front of the basket and peered in at the little stripey face looking out at her.

"Please don't ever do that again," she whispered to Tiger. "Thank you so much for rescuing him," she told Jess's dad.

He grinned at her. "I didn't, Ava! It was all you! I think you'd better take him home and make a big fuss of him."

Ava nodded, picking up the carrier – she didn't even hold it by the handle, she wrapped her arms round it, like she never wanted to let Tiger go. She could feel the kitten padding about inside as she carried him down the path and round the corner to her house. She called goodbye to Jess – she couldn't wave, she was holding on too tight to Tiger in his carrier.

Lucy and Bel followed Ava into the house and crouched down next to her as she put the carrier down on the hall floor. Tiger peered out at them all, his ears twitching.

"It's all right," Ava whispered. "You're home now."

Tiger stepped slowly out of the carrier and then scrambled up on to Ava's knees, purring at last. She had come and rescued him. He'd known she would.

HOLLY WEBB

Holly Webb started out as a children's
book editor and wrote her first series for
the publisher she worked for. She has been
writing ever since, with over one hundred
books to her name. Holly lives in Berkshire,
with her husband and three young sons.
Holly's pet cats are always nosying around
when she is trying to type on her laptop.

For more information
about Holly Webb visit:

www.holly-webb.com